Hello Fellow Dancer,
My name is Ballerina Konora.

I love stories, adventures, and ballet, and I'm glad you're here today!

Will you be my dancing partner and act out the story along with me and Joey?

I've included descriptions of movements that express the story. You can decide whether to use these ideas or create your own moves. Be safe, of course, and do what works for you in your space. And if you want to settle in and enjoy the pictures first, that's fine.

P.S. You don't have to be a kangaroo to act like Joey. Anyone can dance like all of the creatures in this story.

Once upon a dance, Joey Kangaroo was the only kangaroo at the Funville Zoo. He was a kind creature, and he quickly became friends with every animal he met. He especially enjoyed when children visited.

But there was one thing that made Joey sad.

We all feel sad sometimes. Can you remember how it feels to be sad in your body?

My head hangs a little lower, my back gets a little round and slumped. My shoulders lean forward like it's too much effort to hold them up. And my feet feel heavy and tired, like I don't want to pick them up at all.

How would you move if you felt sad like Joey?

The zoo staff and visitors thought perhaps Joey didn't like being locked up, or that he was lonely. But the truth was the kangaroo was terribly upset that he didn't know how to jump.

He remembered his friends springing and bouncing along, but he couldn't quite recall how it was done.

Sometimes Joey would try to jump. He'd try to jump with his head, and sometimes with his arms.

Imagine you're Joey and don't know how to jump. How would you figure out which body parts to use?

Let's be like Joey and try to jump without doing a real jump, first with our head and then with our arms. It's tricky to use only one part at a time. It's amazing how our bodies learn to coordinate so many moving pieces.

Joey would push one foot off the ground at a time, as if a single foot was jumping, and then try the other foot.

Sometimes he would try to jump with his back. Sometimes, with his knees.

And one time, he even tried to jump with his tongue!

But Joey never got off the ground.

Almost as if you're sending the floor away, push one foot off the ground, and then the other foot. Lift your heel off first, and press your toes away using the bottom of your foot.

Using your back, lean forward and come up fast. Bend and bounce your knees. Ballet dancers use these bends so often that we have a special fancy French name for them: *plié*.

Flick your tongue out like a frog trying to catch a fly and then *weeeiich thur tun su ur oohhs* (translation: reach your tongue to your nose). This movement makes me laugh!

Joey decided he would venture out into the wide world and hope to meet his jump.

The kangaroo waited until all the other animals had stretched their stretches and gone to sleep.

Pretend you're one of the zoo animals getting ready to go to bed. Put your arms up high and make your back long. Stretch your arms to the side like an airplane and imagine that your fingertips are being pulled in opposite directions.

Try the move again, this time adding a giraffe side stretch or tilt to your movement.

Next, put your knees on the ground and sit your bottom on top of your feet. Now reach your arms forward and imagine you're a lion getting ready for a long sleep. Then, give a nice, big hippo yawn.

Joey started out marching a happy march as he hurried along, hoping to find his jump soon.

After a while, his march lost its spring, and his steps slowed down. He was getting tired.

Let's march alongside Joey! Lift your knees into the air with each step. It's like we have jumping feet and knees, but no jump.

Now walk quickly. Then make each step slower and slooower, and even slooooowwerrr.

Suddenly, Joey heard music. He followed the sound to a nearby building.

The windows were high, so Joey stretched his neck up, up, up to get a glimpse of what was happening inside.

What do we hear?

Can you stretch up like Joey, and go on your tiptoes?

Sttrrreeeettcchhh your neck as if you were a tall giraffe. Peek inside to see where the music is coming from.

Joey couldn't believe his kangaroo eyes! Inside, there were dancers dancing. And they were jumping!

They jumped with both of their feet together.

They jumped with their feet moving apart and back together.

Let's pretend that we're onstage with the dancers Joey is watching! How can we jump with our feet together? I'm going to pretend to glue my ankles together and put a little tape all around them in my imagination. Can you jump without letting your feet come apart?

Next, jump your feet out **wide.**

The dancers jumped on one foot and then the other. Joey was amazed at how they could have so much power in just one leg!

Let's hop up and down. Stand like a flamingo: keep one foot off the ground. Try to jump keeping your foot in the air. It's a little tricky and might take some practice.

Now try your other foot. Most of us dancers have one leg that is easier to jump on than the other. Do you have a preference?

The dancers skipped around the stage.

Joey's wide eyes darted back and forth, following the dancers' graceful hops.

Skipping is like a march that jumps. Let's hop on one foot, and then hop on the other foot. Imagine you are joyful and keep going: hop, hop, hop, skip, skip, skip. With our happy energy, our hop becomes a little scooch forward.

Then the dancers started making gigantic leaps all around and back and forth across the stage.

Joey was mesmerized!

To make a leap, called a *grand jeté* in fancy French, start on one foot and kick your leg out in front. Imagine you are stepping over a scary, sleeping crocodile. Great! Now try the same thing again, but this time add a little spring off the floor. Keep pretending that you're stepping over something scary.

Suddenly, the little kangaroo felt something inside. It was kind of like a sneeze that is on its way up to your nose. Except this was like a jump sneeze, or maybe a jump hiccup.

Much to Joey's surprise, his feet and his knees and his body all tried to jump at the same time, and Joey went ever so slightly into the air.

Can you make the tiniest jump you've ever made?
Let's make our silly surprised faces.

Then, like another little hiccup, Joey jumped again. And again. And each time the kangaroo jumped, he went a bit higher. Now, Joey was jumping pretty BIG jumps.

Let's do some medium jumps into the air.

Then, Joey did the **BIGGEST** jump of all. It felt like he was going to jump to the moon, he jumped so high.

Can you jump high, too? Picture yourself on a trampoline in the moonlight, looking up toward the moon and getting closer and closer with each jump. I love pretending I'm under the stars, letting go of all my cares and worries.

Maybe we even let out a "Woo Hoo!" or a giant "HA!" as we fly up in the sky!

Well, Joey just kept on jumping, and he jumped all the way to a park across the street. The only time he stopped jumping was to cross the road. He looked ever-so-carefully to one side, then the other, then the other, then the other, before he cautiously stepped off the curb.

Pretend you are looking in every direction. Twist and turn your body so you could even see behind you if you had to.

Over in the park, Joey saw a frog. She was jumping on lily pads, and she started each jump with her arms and legs touching the ground. It looked like she was jumping an even bigger jump than Joey's when her entire body lifted and expanded into the air. Joey could faintly hear her singing a jumping song to herself:

♪ Oh, I like to jump and jump and jump,
and I like to go up high.
I like myself, and I like my jumps
as I fly into the sky! ♪

Try a frog jump from down low. It almost feels like you are f l y i n g !

The frog intrigued Joey, so he introduced himself. He told the frog he'd just learned to jump, and that her jumping skills impressed him.

The frog said her name was Juniper, and that she'd be happy to have a jumping pal.

As Joey jumped alongside her, he realized that all of his sadness had faded away. He had found his jump, and now he jumped, jumped, jumped for joy!

Together, Juniper and Joey jumped back to the Funville Zoo, where they danced happily ever after.

Can you imagine a frog and kangaroo jumping all around together? I've only seen it in my imagination, but it makes me smile.

I bet you have a beautiful smile! I wish I could see it, but I'll have to settle for daydream smiles.

Thee end.

The end.

My grandpa always ended stories this way. I want to share the tradition with you.

Thanks for being my dance partner.

Until our next adventure.

Love,

Konora

We'd be like Joey, and jump for joy, if we got a kind, honest review from a grown-up on Amazon.

We're a mom and daughter pair who were happily immersed in the ballet world until March of 2020. This project has been a labor of love, and it would mean the world to know it made someone happy.

THE DANCE-IT-OUT! COLLECTION

Once Upon a Dance
Series Catalog:
· Dance-It-Out!
· Dancing Shapes
· Konora's Shapes
· Ballet Journals
· Inspiration & Choreography

www.OnceUponADance.com
Watch for Subscriber Bonus Content

Made in the USA
Las Vegas, NV
01 December 2021

35757862R00026